Krakow

A novella

Sean Akerman

Harvard Square Editions
New York
2018

Krakow, by Sean Akerman

ISBN 978-1-941861-57-8
Printed in the United States of America

Published in the United States by
Harvard Square Editions
www.harvardsquareeditions.org

*This book is a work of fiction. References to real
people, events, establishments, organizations, or
locales are intended only to provide a sense of
authenticity, and are used fictitiously. All other
characters, and all incidents and dialogue, are
drawn from the author's imagination and are not to
be construed as real.*

Whatever shadow there was in that world
it was the one each cast
onto the other,
the thin black seam
they seemed to be trying to work away
between them. I held my breath.
As far as I could tell, the work they did
with sweat and light
was good. I'd say
they traveled far in opposite directions.

—Jorie Graham, "Salmon"

An Explanation

THE READER who picks up this book will wonder if I am a thief. How do I live with myself, what with reading strangers' journals?

Let me explain: one year ago, I moved into this apartment in deep Brooklyn. Midwood to be exact. Six floors below is Ocean Avenue, where a rush of traffic moves. Red lights pulse on the Verrazano Bridge several miles away. I have many neighbors in this building, but I struggle to describe them. When they work, if they work, who they are; these are mysteries to me. All I know is that it is very Russian and Hasidic in these parts. The men carry themselves with a heft that says they will never be torn off the earth.

My bedroom faces the back of another building: fire escapes, dead aloe plants, abandoned window boxes, a view of tiled kitchens. This is what I see. The light comes most from the two windows facing Ocean Avenue, which, mid-morning, let in a steady stream of sun lifting the otherwise dour mood of this perch. On the brick wall in the living room, I tacked a tapestry—is it Hindu? Buddhist? I don't know—of an adorned elephant. A friend described the space as spare.

When I moved here, a few large items of furniture were in the main room. An elegant armoire of great girth stood in the bedroom. Half a dozen articles of clothing hung on the hangers. The fridge was partially stocked. I've since appropriated the armoire and liquor cabinet as my own; everything else I tossed, except for what follows. You see, tucked in the far left corner of the bedroom closet were two notebooks—one moleskin, the other a larger notebook with a mahogany color—and inside, large lines like the kind designed for children. I took a cursory glance through the journals, but I didn't make anything of them. So it was easy to forget about them altogether. In fact, there was enough to get used to that I didn't even pause over the apartment itself for many months. It was a place to sleep, make coffee, shower, and cook pasta. Then spring came and I tossed out all the sweaters that the moths tore through. When I lifted the wool, I saw the journals. There they were, one stacked neatly atop the other.

It is hard not to be curious about who lived in an apartment before you. Naturally, you wonder how the last tenants moved through the halls, where they sat, and then you wonder who they were, even before they lived there. So I asked the building super, who made an exploding motion with his hands. In other words, they broke up. And as they were breaking up, they wrote journals. And then they left these journals behind, because why would you ever want to cart these reminders with you after?

First I opened his, then hers, and then I shut them. It felt unethical to read words that someone never intended for another person. Then, several days later, I opened them again and read a few entries before deciding the whole project was out of the question. Back they went into the closet, right where they were, under a new batch of clothing. But one night I couldn't sleep, so I took them out, laid on the floor, and began to read them. They were written in the summer and fall, just a few months before I moved here.

When I discovered the journals, I was working as a writer for a fledgling newspaper in lower Manhattan. The pay was abysmal, and the work itself was no better. Most days I would cover restaurants and bars going out of business because of a corporation larger and more neon buying up the lease, and on better days I would be allowed to review performance art where mimes juggled oranges, or actors just out of college dressed in black and screamed German philosophy at the audience.

The newspaper went out of business and vanished with little notice, disappearing from print and online in a flash. To pay the bills, I have a temp job at an office in upper midtown, making phone calls and laying out extensive spreadsheets. The woman I am filling in for is on maternity leave, but her baby showed up early, meaning I won't have work for much longer.

Once I read the journals, I wondered about the aftermath. Where are these two people now? Do they speak? Are they involved with others? Their names are even mysteries to me. The title I've given to these journals—*Krakow*—comes from the place for which they both longed. It occupies a ghostly destination for them. But then again, to read these at all evokes a ghostly feeling: the slurs said by the radiator's nook, the decisions at the stove. The love they made and lost caked itself to the wall in the style of cigarette smoke, yellowing the space around a framed picture.

Their words echoed with me, having come to New York following a disastrous breakup; in reading the fading away of two strangers, I feel a twinge from wounds that never healed in the first place. Soon I will move again, probably to Queens, where I hear the rent is cheaper. And while these long hard years will recede, I cannot throw away these documents, as much as I don't want to live with them anymore. I never could reject anyone, even strangers.

Yours,
Sean Akerman

[Him]

13 July

I do not know what my life will look like in 90 days. To get a job requires a potent mix of magic and luck. The world this inspires is full of long shadows that grow thinner and taller. A figure moves in the distance, quickly, and disappears behind a building. A dog barks. To share this is impossible.

I wish I could say that when everything you wanted pales away and ends in disaster, you realize that it was just the beginning. But I don't know that. With her, I've become so exhausted talking about it. She says I don't express myself, don't know what I'm feeling, won't share my real struggles. We fought about this again on Friday night, sitting together on the stoop of a building near the Greek restaurant where we had just eaten. (Why am I still paying a share of the bill?)

After spending eight years in radio, I know what my voice means. Most people don't know what their voice means. Mine sinks into a baritone when I have convictions about something and am on the verge of persuading another person to share those convictions. That was the voice I reached for and didn't get.

"What if this doesn't end soon?" I asked her. "What if I cannot find work? You keep assuming things will get better, but from where I sit, it is very possible that they won't."

"What I want to know is what that deep fear is. You keep pouring yourself into these words, but I think you're blocked."

"Blocked?"

"You're walking in the woods with your head down and your focus on the ground in front of you has blurred your vision. If you looked up, you'd see there are many paths."

"Since you can see them, do you want to tell me what they are?"

"Don't be like that. Getting a little perspective on your situation won't kill you."

"Can we talk about a what-if situation though? I run out of money, and then—"

"It's like you walk around forgetting you have willpower. What do you want to have happen?"

"That our life goes on," and I looked at her very seriously as I said it.

"In another age, you would be the guy with the fallout shelter," she said, relaxing her body and checking her phone to see the time.

Eventually we stood up and walked home, where we drank more wine and managed to not continue. It was gone, and by the morning, what was bad seemed as though it had never existed in the first place.

14 July

I swallowed the last of my edible as the train brought me over the Manhattan Bridge. The rain slaked against the window and the lights of lower Brooklyn blurred. Only light and rain—that's all there was. At the other end of the subway car, a woman leaned, half-asleep, who looked like Nina. The electric feeling stayed in my neck, first like a lump, and then it got to my eyes. Now there's a long tingle that shows no sign of stopping. Time off the grid is meant to do what? Freedom to think should not require distance.

16 July

Sometimes, I will be walking home from the subway and the voice of no one in particular will move through the buildings like the wind, raising a question about whether this fits. And it isn't hard to keep walking and focus on something else—a stranger, a bodega, the straight stretch of highway down Ocean Avenue—and keep on with the day.

The first time I had doubts was a month after we met. We were at a hospital in midtown visiting her father, who was going for a check-up to deal with a very painful knee injury. He was howling in pain to the point that he had to be pumped full of Naproxen. This is how we were introduced to each other, which is not ideal. I actually choked on my own words and mumbled my name, plus the first few sentences. He was not coherent either, and when I looked over at her, she glassed us as though we were two unknown creatures.

Then we all went out to lunch at a restaurant none of us liked. It was a French place not far from the hospital, with white tablecloths and lighting fixtures that were meant to imitate the gas lamps of Paris. When you are struggling to connect with another person, it does not help to have food that is curated on your plate as though it is competing for a blue ribbon, and you sit there, the most uncomfortable judge. I ordered a burger. The gruyere plus the grease from the meat trickled out of the bun and spilt to my thigh, an act of gravity that everyone saw but no one commented on. He and I tried to talk to no avail. One part of it was all the pain meds, another part of it was me being nervous, which turns me into a terrible interviewer. The most unsayable part was whatever existed between the two of them, a closeness that made me feel like a violation.

By the time we returned to my apartment that night, the strain was gone. The strain could always go away once we were alone. My roommate had left for the summer and she was there at least five nights a week. We made a habit of eating dinner on the floor. I read out loud to her the last few pages of Garcia Marquez's *Love in the Time of Cholera* and she smiled, supine, at hearing my voice break a little at the last few lines.

17 July

I won't continue to live like this. I stormed out of the apartment this morning, circled the block, and finally bought toilet paper, juice, and tonic water from the bodega. The short, stunning Israeli woman who works the register looked at me, apology in her eyes, as though she was trying to give some sympathy to me for the struggles I present without words each time I buy necessities. Afterward, I sat on a stoop and smoked a cigarette. An elderly Russian woman said go away, these are not your stairs.

This is how it started: I said I must start repaying my loans, the deferment period is over, can you help with this for a bit? Silence. She looked away. Those loans were from the time before we knew each other, she said, and how would you feel if the shoe was on the other foot? I'd help, I said. I don't care about money. Yes, she said, but one of us must. From there, we pulled away from each other like a wishbone.

My unemployment totals eleven hundred a month. When rent is paid, groceries are purchased, after the stray dinner out, less than a hundred dollars is left. Her work pays three times that right now. My father said I shouldn't ask her. Now I wish I hadn't. But when we are lying awake at seven a.m., laughing about the neighbor who plays the trumpet so poorly, it feels impossible that there is a limit to what we have.

"Keep looking for work and try to negotiate for a longer deferment," she said.

"Keep looking? What do you think I do every day?"

"Baby, I understand you're frustrated. But you might have to be open to other opportunities."

"I went to school, got a degree, got a second degree, and now I'm supposed to throw that out the window?"

"No one's throwing anything out the window. But do you know how much is out there? Take what you can get. Look, if that means lugging pipes as they dig out the Second Avenue subway—what's not noble about that? You might not even know your own vastness."

"I know I've had a career in radio that I've worked for, so forgive me if manual labor doesn't sound appealing. This has nothing to do with vastness."

"I tend bar two nights a week and it feeds beautifully into the art I do."

"It must be nice to have started in this life with the support—and I mean that in all ways—to follow your bliss to the extent that anyone with actual problems looks like they're whining."

"What you're talking about is a matter of perspective," she said, but her words were shaky.

"And you've been spared from a lot, so don't prescribe to me."

"Then I don't know what to say. Yes, it'd be lovely if the man I loved had work. I'm sorry things have not worked out the way you intended. I'm sorry you were laid off for no good reason."

"But on some level, you believe it's a just world, right? You think whether or not things work out are a matter of how bad a person wants it, right?"

"Well, to an extent, isn't it?"

In the air outside, I thought of Nina. I thought of our makeshift dinners and the cheap beer we toasted on her fire escape. And the evening a condom broke and Plan B was outrageously priced, so we just hoped, and the worst didn't happen. A stretch of homes on Avenue N was slate gray with gingkoes placed between each building. It was even enough to imagine I was elsewhere. I pictured running into Nina on the platform at Houston Street, her effusiveness, us not sure what to say, then Nina telling her, You've got a really great guy here, and if I were you, I'd try to hold on to that relationship. Because I didn't, and I'm ruined for that reason.

I don't even remember where I went. Streets with nothing but two-story homes overwhelmed me. I called a few people but none of them picked up, so I leaned against a telephone pole and checked my email. A half hour later she texted me and asked if I wanted to get a drink.

I know that we came close to an ending, and although it did not happen, I cannot shake the feeling that it is near.

We agreed to meet at the bar six blocks away, which we go to once a week because they have a good happy hour. I saw her from afar breathing the deflated breaths of a post-fight, yet she was also managing okay. Before she saw me, I studied her and remembered how much of her life took place in other countries, in other states. There she was, leaning a little and fiddling with the straw to her gin and tonic. Fighting with her partner, sitting alone in a bar, figuring it out—these things all fit her so well. Why don't they fit me so well? I ordered a beer and watched a baseball game unfold. Then I went over and sat on the same side of the booth where she was.

"If I'm not the person you want, just tell me. It doesn't mean there's anything wrong with you or me. Most relationships don't work out," she said.

As she spoke, a few slow tears came down the right side of her face. Then mine. I said no, let's try to work this out. You are the person I want. Can we just go home, please? I don't want to be out tonight.

26 July

It is six p.m. and I am sitting on my aunt's porch in an Adirondack chair after a hike up to Bash Bish Falls. There, on the Massachusetts border, the land begins to rise, and somewhere far north, a deep reservoir exists that creates the waterfall I saw split in two by a giant, arrowhead-shaped rock. Today, it was thunderous. Streams of cold spilt fast and slammed down onto a placid, greenish pool where dozens of locals and tourists gathered to take pictures and feel the mist that sprayed in the air.

As we sat in their backyard late at night with citronella candles burning, throwing cherry pits over the fence, it occurred to me that my feet on the grass and the cool air moving through my shirt and the looseness and happiness on my aunt's face, made for one of the more meaningful moments of the summer. You come to a place, you participate in other people's habits and conversations, you sleep in new beds, you see roads that are not the everyday ones, and little by little, you are not reduced.

We ate skirt steaks with grilled eggplant and peppers, tapenade and half ears of premature corn. I looked over at her, happy, eating corn like her mouth was a typewriter. They asked questions about my job search, and I said I was still sending out lots of applications, I was hopeful, but also exhausted. Fireflies lifted above our talk, first in a way that mesmerized us, and then quickly they became absorbed into the landscape. This, I said to myself, is what it's like to bring someone you love to other people you love. You serve as a bridge, and although you would have more fun talking to each one alone, the fact that strangers build something out of you and you alone is enough to send a warm pulse all through your body. My aunt and her wife talked about a trip they were about to take to Scotland, how Scotland has relics of the Vikings, my ancestors. And we talked about the trip we had taken a year ago to Poland and Hungary.

29 July

She got home late last night as I was trying to fight off the urge to sleep. A heavy sensation took over that left no bridge between the seconds: one instant, deep dream sleep, the next, a focused study of the paintings on the wall. Then, she took off her clothes with dregs of light spilling in from above the stove. The whites of her eyes glowed, too. Her hair is exceptionally long now.

Déjà vu. The first night we slept together, the same pose. I was fumbling to take off my boots and pants and then she turned to me, shorn of all her clothes, looking like the first person of all time, stepping onto the moss out of the forest. Arms loose on her sides with silver bracelets slid all the way down to her wrist. We embraced and her hair felt like silk, with its dark brown color in my face.

"Are you up?" she asked.

"I am."

No words other than a mutual I love you halfway through, at the same time. Afterward, we stayed atop the duvet with a hand on each other's chest, listening to National Public Radio. A lead singer from The Mountain Goats explained his heroin addiction.

I went into the bathroom and studied the slight chafing marks left on me. Clicking the light brought a measure of pain to my head. All over, I felt ragged. Red marks so red a bare spill of blood was about to start. My hair had gone crazy, with sudden bangs, and my eyes were bloodshot.

When she dozed off, I went outside to the bodega to buy cigarettes. The air was liquid and smooth. Hardly any cars sped by, despite the avenue being a major thruway. The super was washing the area next to the steps with a solution lush with chemicals.

"Late night alone?" he asked.

"Yes," I told him.

6 August

I wonder: is she reading these entries? I have the journal tucked in my desk, in the locked drawer, but she knows where the key is. I know she writes, too.

This weekend we celebrated our anniversary. She said she wanted to take me out, and that I couldn't pay for anything. We rode a bus all the way to Bedford Avenue where the streets were clogged with a post-work crowd, none of them dressed in business attire, all quite hip. Come this way, she said, I have a surprise. She took my hand and led me through a restaurant's narrow opening where we slid past drinkers with their elbows out. Then, the narrowness ended and we were in a resplendent garden with pebbles lining the ground, small green tables and crooked chairs. Spider plants overhung next to gas lamps. See, this is just like New Orleans, she said. Just like it. Don't you remember? Look around.

A waitress pointed to our table and I went to the bathroom. As soon as the door shut, I threw a wash of cold, hard water up to my face to quell the burning that was starting behind my eyes. What will my life be like without her? None of this. Fewer dinners out. Fewer words spoken in the course of the day.

Most of the cocktails were made with absinthe. So when I had two in quick succession, I felt very light, at least 15 pounds lighter, with a slight buzzing in my ears. Each time, we lifted our glasses up and studied the contents like scientists before toasting to nothing in particular. And because we were in a place that modeled itself after New Orleans, we began to talk about the things that we liked there.

When we went to New Orleans, we had been dating only three months. The plane flew over Lake Pontchartrain, an enormous, brackish body of water with a causeway cutting through its middle, so long that at certain points you cannot see land. Out in the hotel's garden, we drank coffee, ate beignets, and walked through the French quarter, all the way to a cemetery, with the tombs above ground. Don't go in there, a man said to us. People get robbed in there. We looked at him, wide-eyed, and then went back to the more touristy section until it was night, when we crossed a thruway into the Faubourg Marigny neighborhood. Streets slanted sideways and trailed off into homes with long driveways, ramshackle places that people had lived in for a long time. When the rain started, we went inside a bar that was nearly empty. It was almost all dark, lit only by candles. A jazz singer crooned a Billie Holiday tune.

We danced in the middle of the room, feeling the tremor of her voice move through us.

Of course, I woke up around four a.m., as is the case when I overdo it with the hard stuff. There was not even a shred of bitterness between us to think about. I came into the living room and clicked on my computer, checked the news for a second, my email, and then Facebook. I searched Nina's profile, and she had changed her picture. Now she is sitting on a rock with a knit cap over her head, a jean vest and a tank top, wearing the same wide, goofy smile she wore when I was in love with her four years ago. That long since I last saw her? Yes. She was passing through New York and needed a place to stay for the night. At the time, it felt like the greatest evening of my life. Maybe still? Snow had started to spin around when we left a wine bar near Prospect Park. With the light so bare because of the overcast sky, we walked into the park, poaching in the dark, and threw snowballs at each other, tackled each other to the ground, and laid down watching a vortex of snow.

At my apartment, we slept face to face, not touching, not talking, just looking, and fading into a heavy sleep. Another person's eyes closing as your own close—how rare is that? There were things she never said to me, but since I remember the arc of her voice, I can imagine her saying those things. I started a few messages to her but erased them all. Maybe I'll send this one.

Dear Nina,

We haven't spoken in over two years, and lately that's caused me some pain. Tell me what your life looks like these days in Vancouver. Ever make it back east? If I came west, would you have me?

8 August

They came yesterday. Her father and her brother, Hayden, arrived at one p.m. sharp and spent the first five minutes congratulating themselves on maintaining military punctuality even though those years are long gone. The plan was that we would work together to help hoist into the apartment an armoire that once belonged to her grandfather. But when I opened the door, they had lugged it up on their own.

"Not bad, eh?" her father said to me, out of breath.

"You guys could have buzzed me," I told Hayden.

"Don't worry about it. You've got other things to do."

They moved past me and embraced her while I stood cross-armed and assessed the new furniture that would live in my home. It was taller than me at a shade over six feet, with two copper handles and metal hinges crafted with ornate swirls. Her father said it belonged to his father almost a century ago in Odessa. The family carried it by ship when they emigrated to the U.S. Hayden interrupted before the history became extensive and drew me into the kitchen to see if I had any beer on hand. Yeah, go for it, you deserve it, I told him. He handed me one, too, and we toasted while looking out the small window into an airshaft.

Hayden is the most positive person I have ever met. When I look at him, I see echoes of her in his facial structure, and I have to pull back a little, because I find her so attractive. He enters every situation with the feeling that he is getting along beautifully with each person, and then, in fact, he does. Around him, I smile more than normal and talk right away about what's on my mind. I am never certain he listens, but he does offer encouragement and raises his eyebrows to smirk quite often, which makes me feel that we are in on some ruse together.

Her father leaned into the kitchen and waited for us to stop talking before he spoke.

"Hey chief, what's the good word in radio?" he asked me.

"What's that?" I said.

I never seemed to understand what he was saying.

"Jobs. Any news?"

"Looking every day, but this seems to be the slow season."

"Isn't radio going the way of the dodo? Aren't podcasts all the rage now?"

"Well, yes and no. Podcasts are kind of democratic—anyone can set that up, but there's no money there. Radio takes a little more finesse."

He shrugged his shoulders to eliminate my comment and said, "Gotta stay ahead of the curve," as he disappeared into the living room.

The next hour lagged. Having family members visit you in a small apartment is never easy, because no one knows where to sit, what there is to look at never takes very long, and before you know it, you start to feel oppressed by these strangers so near to the intimacy of your life. After a while, she left the room for what felt like a month to make coffee for herself and her father. Hayden spoke of his architecture work but digressed fast, knowing that jobs were a touchy subject in our house. I spoke of the hurricanes I heard about on the news and wondered if one of them would make it this far north.

"You got out of the hard part. Want to lend a hand for the finale?" her father asked me.

"Of course he does," she said.

The three of us edged our fingers around the sides of the armoire, then began to walk it into the bedroom. We tottered back and forth, trying to not catch our feet on the rug, and felt the cedar pull on our tendons. Her father smiled at me for what I believe was the first time in our history. I smiled back at him, but my gaze was fixed over his shoulder, where I could see down to the street. A Greyhound bus cruised by. More than anything, I wanted to be there, headed to where I could start fresh.

13 August

The film she had worked on was premiering at Landmark Sunshine down in the Village tonight. She was coming from her friend's play in Morningside Heights, so she asked that I bring her black dress, which I didn't really look at when I stuffed it in a plastic bag. But when I got there, and when she changed into it, I couldn't believe how gossamer it was, why would she want to parade around in something like that, with her back almost bare, an exceptionally short cut to it and a chain serving as the primary strap. A chain. She made the rounds, off and on introducing me as her boyfriend, but for the most part, I was a wallflower.

An Australian man, tall with a jagged chin and dark eyes, was the only person I cared to talk to. He explained a play he was writing—people being forced to talk about their sex lives—and I feigned interest. I talked about a radio program I wanted to produce and he half-listened. Quickly, we wolfed down several beers before the lights dimmed. I couldn't find her, so I sat with the Australian man. Jean-Paul was his name.

Halfway through the film, my phone buzzed with the text message "I see you." Through the dark of the theater I scanned for her but all the heads looked the same. I have known her for two years, and still I could not begin to find her profile. The number of women with brown hair and Eastern European heritage several generations back, with high cheekbones and an aquiline nose, is startling.

Then I saw her. The next row over, many seats down. Her face was turned toward me, smiling in an exaggerated way, as though she had done something wrong. I smiled back and turned toward the film. It didn't leave an impression on me. I could tell that the cinematography was sharp, which gladdened me because that was her work, but the story was lacking, the acting was overdone. Two high school students dabble into alcoholism, see each other through their parents' divorces, and one night, while quite intoxicated, they have sex. Much of the film deals with the aftermath of the event. The lights came up and I sighed to Jean-Paul.

When we exited in the main area, she walked toward me and gave me a large, public kiss that made me pull my head back. This is Axel, she said, and he's the DP. He saved me a lot. I shook his hand and studied how foreign he looked. He was tall, about my height, yet his body was gaunt, and his face had a shape and coloring to it that placed him somewhere between French and Spanish.

"My people are Basque," he said to me, noticing me look. "In case you're wondering."

"I was."

The whole time he had his hand on her shoulder, which meant her bare shoulder.

"I must know, what are your opinions on the film? She says you have good taste. And I know she wouldn't select a man with poor taste."

At that, she spotted someone she knew and

walked to the other side of the room while my mouth hung open.

"The script was great," I said after a pause. "And the film itself had its moments."

"Ah, I hear the critical groundhog poaching for his shadow."

"The what?"

"It's a phrase we use on set. She'll explain, I'm sure. Go on. And don't worry about hurting me. Just say what you feel."

I said my criticisms of the film, but I don't remember the words leaving my mouth. The autopilot went on while the rest of me wondered how much he knew about our troubles. He definitely knew something. And of course, I had done the same with countless friends, but none of them—not a single one—would show an intimation to her of knowing about it. It was not that I wanted to pretend such conversations didn't exist between them, for I knew they did. What I wanted was the etiquette of him pretending such conversations never happened.

Now, I knew there were no safeguards. Anything could happen. We could come undone in public and others would watch, expecting it.

"And this vivacious woman assisted with the

casting," Axel said to me, placing his hand on the wrist of a woman passing by, no older than 22. He lingered too long with that touch, as well, enough to convince me that he operated on the principle of what he thought men were like. Given, he couldn't have been older than 29. How he cultivated his clothing—the hem of his jeans, the fall of his shirt cuff beyond the suit jacket, the narrowness of his tie—reeked of self-consciousness. Yet it also reeked of wealth, a vision drawn from spending years around parents who traveled the world.

"I must bid farewell to an old friend," I told him, using words I never used, but feeling the need to meet his pretensions as I watched Jean-Paul drunkenly glaze the room for the exit.

"There will be many more of these openings," he said. "We'll cross paths again, I'm sure."

I nodded and walked toward Jean-Paul, who was almost cross-eyed with a feline smile taking up his face. He mumbled something and went to lean against the wall, but it was further away than he anticipated, leading to a loud thud that drew everyone's attention.

"Are you hanging in there?" I asked him.

He smiled again and made a big breath.

"Time to go home," he said. "I'm smashed."

"We'll walk you out. Where are you going?"

He slurred his words again and said something about the sea. Coney Island was what he meant. Great, I said, you can come with us. We're going that way, too.

The three of us left and walked to the F train on Houston Street. Southern-like heat washed over us as not a single subway came for a long time. The ceilings were lower than any other station, too. My white shirt had changed color with a butterfly pattern of sweat making the outline of my chest hair. She was glistening in the way many women rarely sweat, looking more uncomfortable than on the verge of collapse. She and I talked a little about the film, but most of our attention went to Jean-Paul, who swung between banal anecdotes about Brisbane and being morose.

"Did you like Axel?" she asked me when the train pulled out of the drab light of the Canal Street stop and moved into the bluish black sky on the Manhattan Bridge.

It was the first time a skyline view inspired nothing good in me. The question was meant to pull out my discomfort with Axel, his pseudo-European ways, and most of all, it was meant to start a fight, because she already knew what I thought of Axel, and she herself must have been uncomfortable with him, but she wanted me to say it.

"I like Jean-Paul," I told her, putting my hand on the shoulder of the drunk man who was leaning on me, and looking straight into her eyes with more aggression than I had conjured in a long time. She was ready to sob and I didn't care. Recently, drinking gave me the freedom to not care when she was close to such moments. Recently, it made me incite those moments.

"Why are you doing this?" she asked.

"Doing what?"

Jean-Paul made a loud hiccup and then fell into a sneezing fit. He claimed that we were great in between the billows of snot he shot forth, some of which landed on his knee, others on the beige subway floor, and still others into the ether. I told him that he was sneezing because his body was rejecting the amount of alcohol he poured into it, that lots of people have this reaction. Alcohol prevents the breakdown of histamine, which leads to allergy-like symptoms. Sneezing, red skin, heart palpitations. You'll be fine, Jean-Paul, I said.

He wasn't listening. He fixed his sight out the window on the empty yards of houses we passed, looking back as though he had missed something important.

24 August

I woke up at four forty-five this morning, not because of a dream or alcohol's exit, and went to the bathroom where two tears streaked slowly from my eyes into the sink, smelling of salt. I looked at myself in the mirror and didn't know what was happening.

Around first light, I fell into a deep doze that only ended when she left for work and the bell clanged a little upon the door slamming shut. She has no grace when she exits. I sat up and watched the neighbors resist the day by blasting their air conditioners high. I went over and turned on our window fan, but the fear of inhaling the dust overcame me, so I turned it off and said forget making this environment artificial, I'm fine sweating. Out in the kitchen, I learned that she had swallowed all but a teaspoon of the coffee, so I had to make another pot. When I lifted the espresso maker off the stove, its bottom was still hot, scalding my palm to the point of a low rising blister. You want to believe improvement is impossible, but then little things happen that set you off.

24 August. It didn't click with me until I stared at

the calendar for a moment. Two years on the dot since I last spoke to my mother. I don't know where she is or how she is doing. My parents divorced, my communication with her diminished, and she began a new life. She moved to Chicago, where she had always wanted to live, and moved in with a roommate. Once, we Skyped, and she resembled someone else. Her mannerisms were newly formed and her list of friends was enormous. The talk went one way: she never asked how I was. Instead, she listed the bands she had seen in the last month and said how open people were compared to the more rural places she had lived in Illinois. Later, her roommate contacted me and said their living situation was untenable. My mother's swings in moods and behavior were dramatic, and the police had been phoned several times due to arguments in the night. Was there something I could do? I said I'm sorry, I didn't know she was like that, I hope she gets well soon. Her roommate wrote again and said they were parting ways. She gave me the information of a social worker she hoped would help. But when I phoned the social worker, he said he had many cases and it wasn't his top priority.

The sense of being orphaned is easier to take living in this city. I said this to her a year and a half ago when we sat atop our still-packed boxes in the living room, splitting a bottle of wine. It was one of the only times a thought struck me, because I truly didn't see it coming. I said, "My mother is out there and her life is full of a lot of suffering I don't know about. If I lived anywhere else, with anyone else, I think it'd be terrible to deal with. But it feels okay here. I have you, we have this place, and already everything seems so full." She leaned over and kissed me. From then on, she would check in with me to see if I felt the same way. And for a long time, I did. But neither of us have talked about our families for the last few months, and I can't figure out why.

29 August

The last tenants left behind a few gallons of mustard yellow paint under the sink, and when we found them, we decided that we would scrape away the damaged sections of the wall, repair them with spackle, sand them, and put on a few coats of the paint. We awoke at eight a.m. and I went out to get bagels, she made coffee, and we were up on the step stool by nine. From my laptop, I set all the Rolling

Thunder Revue albums to play. Over us came the sounds of Bob Dylan and his band at their best: clear lyrics, versions of songs never before played with such gusto, the arc of the crowd in the background, filling our apartment with more noise than it had in a long time. The spackle caked itself to our hands, and with our hands we touched each other's faces, making a paste not unlike the kind Dylan had as he performed in those large stadiums in the 1970s. And once it was on our faces, we were free to sing along louder and louder, to the point that all we were doing was singing.

When the spackling was done, we had to wait 30 minutes for it to dry.

"What do you want to do? Stir the paint?" I asked.

She looked at me and one of her eyebrows went up on purpose. So rarely she allowed herself to flirt with me, but that was what she doing.

"Okay."

On the large drop cloth that covered half the length of the living room, we made love. But the mood of it didn't linger into the rest of the morning. In the afternoon, we lathered the walls, paid close attention to the cutting around the baseboard, and looked at the room in new, startling light as the sun went down, the dregs of it shimmering off the yellow, playing against the brick. We crossed our arms and studied the living room, leaning into each other. The space was ours. The liquor cabinet, the coffee table, the desk—these were items we found on the street near the end of the first month we lived here. Although they are not ours, they have become ours—the chips in the wood, the varnishing—so much so that it is impossible to imagine a time when they were not here. The fact is these are our things and that ties us together in a way I never anticipated. My father once said, "Only buy a rug together if you're in it for the long haul."

12 September

Woke up this morning, on the occasion of turning 32, to this message in my Facebook message inbox:

Hello, old friend! I miss you. You've caught me at an interesting intersection of life right now. I am in the process of moving out of the apartment I've lived in for the last two and a half years. And where am I moving to? Over to the Marpole neighborhood, where I believe my people will be.

I am so happy to hear from you. Are you feeling the need for some majestic port gazing and market strolls any time soon? If so, Vancouver is the place to come for a visit. I don't have a home just yet, but I will soon. My dog, Hannah, is having the time of her life in the expanses nearby. As you might remember, my dream is to get a place with a nice patch of land so I can start my own big garden and have more space to breathe. One day.

Are you and your lady still together? Are you married!? Yuri and I were great, though we parted ways a few months ago. It was a difficult decision, considering how long we had known each other. In the time since, I have been trying to take the space and effort to care for myself and figure out what I need.

Here I am sitting on my fire escape with iced tea right now. My back is sore from moving all weekend, but I feel peaceful inside. It's absolutely beautiful here, sunny and in the high 70s. I wish you were here to have a face-to-face chat. I think about you from time to time and easily picture you roaming the streets of NYC. How are your parents doing? Last I heard from you, they were going through a divorce...perhaps happier on the other side now?

We float in and out of each other's consciousness like the tide. That's not a bad thing. There's got to be a reason why we keep returning. At least for me, I have always thought of you with fondness, wonder, and similar pangs of missing. I might be coming out east this winter. And I think I might stay in New York when I do (perhaps not with you, though, because, well...). Obviously, you're at the top of the visiting list. So many friends are growing up and moving away, there are fewer and fewer ties in those old haunts. I am relieved you are holding it down out there. If you ever need a break from the scene, I am going to keep a special place in the park where we can have that stroll.

Now, I know you have more to share...I'll be here when you find the time.

~Nina

18 September

Thirty thousand feet below, I can see the shape of the Hudson Valley, the press of the river around woodlots, with white homes at the end of cul-de-sacs, and chimney smoke heading up toward me. I am on my way back from Montreal looking over the most verdant stretch of land I have ever seen. Below looks like another century.

I haven't slept in 24 hours, but I don't feel tired. In fact, I'm strung with an energy that shows no

signs of ending. I came north with my friend, Henry,
who was slated to talk at an academic conference.
Despite the problems I have on the home front, I
went anyway. And however much we wanted a
sedate few days, that went downhill fast.

Last night, we made our way through the parts of
the city layered with cobblestones and off-kilter
streets. We found a bar with a high, sweeping ceiling
that brewed its own beer in a generous space laid
out like a warehouse, with barrels as tables. Pitcher
after pitcher of strong amber lager left us light and
confessional. Our faces grew red and our eyes less
intense. Declarations of brotherhood started a rise
of tears that never came to fruition. By nine p.m.,
we found a strip club because of the bartender's
recommendation: Cleo's. Bad red lettering shone
above the entrance and a bouncer, around 300
pounds, checked IDs. Inside was the smell of dust.
The stage was shaped like spilt milk. We watched
the girls dance for a while until he took off into one
of the private booths with a short, Middle Eastern
woman named Lily. Enviously, I watched her hands
and calves move behind the curtain, and when
I turned back, a tall woman with dark hair was
standing in front of me. She stared at me, as I was a
deer in the headlights, not her, and continued to

watch as she walked onto the stage and danced for five minutes. When the song ended, she walked over to my table.

"Dylan," she said, extending her hand.

"Like Bob Dylan. Good name."

"Or Dylan Thomas."

"Do you like his books?"

"Do you want a dance?"

"I do."

She led me to the private booth beside Henry, removed all her clothes right away, and began to sashay when the music started. Her long tussled hair covered my face, running a strange, new smell over me: cinnamon. At that, I was gone. I put my hands around her waist and began to kiss her. And then her hips began to move, grinding on my jeans to the point of pain. It had been two years since I'd kissed another woman. A long scar ran the length of her coxal bone with the feel of thread. On her right shoulder, there was a tattoo of a flower without the coloring. When she threw back her hair, I leaned close and smiled at her. She had deep-set dark eyes and a large nose between high cheekbones. She smiled back at me.

"You're cute."

"I'm out of money."

"What a shame."

"In fact, I think I have to borrow a few bucks from my friend. Hold on, he's right over there."

I walked to Henry, explained that I went overboard, and he handed me a few bucks, which I promptly gave to her, along with effusive thanks. She held on to the ends of my fingers for a moment and thanked me, too, biting her lower lip.

"Here's my email address in case you ever come to New York," I told her, writing it down on the back of a receipt. "And I wrote down my phone number, too."

"Thanks," she said.

She smiled and walked away after she read the address, stuffing it in her bustier with the force of a grocery receipt.

"We're not done," Henry said. "I have an idea."

His plan was to visit a student party at McGill University, 20 minutes away. We walked toward the quadrangles in the northern part of town, laughing at a fast clip. By the time we arrived at McGill, I had no desire to go to any party, no desire for anyone. Yet I didn't say that I would prefer to nurse a beer with him at a deserted bar. I said exaggerated things about how excited I was, because I saw that he was unhinged in his enjoyment, and to reel him in was out of the question for the simple reason of friendship.

The party amounted to nothing other than banal conversations with reasonably attractive 20-year-olds about the differences between Canada and America. At one a.m., she sent me a text message saying Good night I love you & miss you terribly, which I responded to with, And you. Through me went a sharp pain of dread that must have changed the look on my face. My mouth turned down, I bit my lower lip, and my breathing became visible from far away. Henry saw me and whispered, Let's get out of here.

So we walked along the northern sections of Montreal for an hour until we came to an expansive park without any signs of life. Talking about everything and anything took up our breath. A decade of friendship with so many nights and meals and beers shared that he has become ingrained into my life as few do, with as much forgotten as remembered. A stream spilt forth from the gutter we paused over. The leaves were beginning to shed from the trees, piling as a momentary dam. Astringent Canadian air rushed over us, making us button our jackets. Then he said good things about her, about how important she was to my life, how she loved me, and how there are ultimately few occasions in time when we can say we love another person. No one will ever be everything, he added. And I said yes, I agree, you're right. This is a small struggle and it will pass.

While he slept, I walked outside the hotel and bought a pack of cigarettes across the street. The night sky became milky, only a hint of wind moving through. It was two thirty a.m. I opened my phone and scrolled down the list of contacts until I came to N, and then I pressed Nina's name, figuring it was eleven thirty on the west coast, and maybe not too late for a talk. After five rings, she picked up. She didn't recognize my voice, and then she did, making a long pause as though she was sucking in all the air in the room. And then, perhaps because it was nighttime, we talked in low whispers, not even about our lives, but about what was going on in front of us. The slow crawl of cars and people in the old town of Montreal. The buzz of an ambulance far outside her window, and the way the trees came together to make a triangle shape that framed perfectly another window, where two people danced.

22 September

The apartment is lonely without her here, because let's face it, half the life has been subtracted. Tonight she is staying at Lisette's house near Prospect Park.

Maybe tomorrow night, too. I cannot imagine the things that are being said about me right now.

On the floor are shards of the wine glass she smashed. She wasn't even drinking out of it; she actually took it out of the cabinet, held it up against the light in the kitchen, and smashed it as she turned her face away. It broke in the gymnastics of slow motion. Considering that I gave her the glass two years ago as a gift, I can't decide whether her gesture was meant to hurt me or whether she hoped a piece would nick an artery.

I said I've been talking to Nina, and I have doubts now. I said it in a voice of certainty, not a statement with uneven footing, but as a fact that had already been established, and I was informing her, in an obligatory way, of the news. As I sat on the couch and bent my head toward the floor like an ashamed dog, I explained that I had just made out with a dancer in Montreal. A look of horror and amazement planed over her face, like she had just received a telegram of war from a country she had never heard of.

She burst into tears and fell into her own lap. I sat there studying her, unable to put even a hand on her shoulder. What dancer? she asked. I just shook my head and walked into the other room, climbed on the fire escape and lit a cigarette. Her face became redder than ever. And I guess this means you want to get back together with you know who? she asked, but I just shook my head.

"You're not doing this to me!" Her body was cartoonish when she said it, taut and leaning toward me, her jaw more open than ever. No one had ever felt so close to hitting me.

A strange calm moved through my body, the feeling of shade on a hot day. And it's still with me. I'm back on the fire escape, having gone through most of a pack of Marlboro blacks.

24 September

My father phoned around the time I got in tonight. He wanted to make sure the check he sent me arrived, and it did, meaning that I'll have rent for October, at least. Then, who knows. Of course, he is also worried about me, but his worry is braided with a great deal of optimism. The few times he met her, he got along with her, found her charming, yet remained convinced that there was too much space between us. On the phone, I told him that I was back in touch with Nina, which he heard without making any judgment other than to remind me that this was not a choice between one woman or the other.

"You could go to the corner bodega and meet someone who changes the whole game," he said when I was silent for a spell. He was referring to the stunning Israeli woman he remembered from when he came to visit last spring. "And that's not to say you should go do that. I'm ultimately saying that you'll be all right."

We said goodbye and I stayed on the couch for an hour, realizing that he had a post-mortem take. This is over. I can't remember what the world looks like without her.

27 September

Only yesterday, after I received a text from Lisette that read She is returning soon. Please try, did I begin to quiver. It was the longest we had gone without seeing each other. She looked like a tourist when she entered the apartment, dressed casually with her large sunglasses and duffel, standing in the doorway.

"You're back," I said, coming out of the bedroom.

"Uh-huh," and her breath heaved, pre-sob.

She began to walk past me until I reached out

and hugged her. Her body felt thinner, smaller—
could that be true in just five days' time? The scent
of her clothes was so ingrained into my life that I
saw them as childhood objects. For a moment I
registered what it would be like if she hadn't come
back. A living death. Stale. Open?

"May I?" she asked, leaning away from me. "I
need a shower."

"Sure. And if you want company, just let me
know," I said, but she didn't respond.

Soon we would have to talk about it. How that
would play out, I wasn't sure. The burn of dread,
which tasted metallic, filled me. Once I could not
have been happier that this woman, whose face was
inches from mine, would sleep next to me for god
knows how many years, that we might someday
create a child together, that there was a secret
language all our own to make.

Now, that future had been gutted. Soon, I knew,
she would come out of the shower and we would sit
on the couch and begin to talk amid very strained
silences, and at first our tones would be even, but
that would turn, and then there would be yelling,
declarations made, octaves that would send my blood
pressure through the roof. This was unavoidable. So
when she came out of the shower, I went to the

couch and resumed my job search. And as soon as she sat down with her hair still dripping, I showed her the radio job I had discovered that promised a high wage, located just south of San Francisco.

"Remember, you liked it out there?"

"That's far," she said.

And it began.

"How's Lisette?"

"She's good. She also thinks you're lacking in some pretty major ways."

"Well, she's sleeping with the father of the boy she nannies for, so let's not use her judgment."

Lisette, like me, came from the Midwest. She was quite smart and thought that most couples were living in some form of a delusion. Every conversation I had with her, I left feeling smarter and a little more critical of the world. That she thought I was lacking pinched me, because I didn't actually mistrust her judgment.

"Do you want to start?" I asked her.

"Start? What could you possibly mean by 'start'? You want me to outline my argument like some district attorney? I won't. I'm here to hold up a mirror to your idiocy. If you think I need to list the reasons why I love you, we have a problem. Actually, I would like you to 'start' by describing this early version of a mid-life crisis you seem to be going through."

"I kissed another woman. You don't think that's a problem?"

"You kissed a stripper. Yeah, I think that's a problem. My boyfriend has self-control issues. Has this ever happened before?"

"No, never," and I looked straight at her, horrified at the thought.

"Was she prettier than me?"

"No, of course not."

"Then why? You tell me why. Don't just shake your head like some big, dumb dog. You come home and you tell me that you are communicating with your ex-girlfriend, but how am I supposed to take this? Does it mean that you still love her and not me?"

I couldn't say. I looked around as though the answer would appear like a video game bubble promising new life. She waited patiently with the corners of her mouth turned down and her eyes kindly fixed upon me. And even though she gave me all the silence and space necessary in order to answer, I could not say anything, so I got up and went to the kitchen, poured us two glasses of water and set them on the coffee table. Then she began to tremble, her stern voice fading into what sounded like skips on a record. The tears were falling right on her thighs.

"You can't tell me. And you know what? So be it. I will continue to love you and be with you, and we can work through this blip on the radar. But that is what it is: a blip. So you will not leave and condemn me."

"Condemn you?"

"My family would never forgive you. You cannot possibly assume that we'd stay together."

"I am not interested in pleasing them."

"Oh, of course not. You could never be bothered to show up for them anyway."

"No one will ever penetrate that force field."

"Care to elaborate, professor?"

"What is there to say? It's as obvious as the sun."

Her top teeth bit her lower lip and she closed her eyes to regain some composure.

"For the love of god, am I speaking Greek? Do you understand what you are taking away? You are blowing up your own life. Your parents divorced, you lost your job, and now you want to burn what is left. That's me. I'm what's left. Yes, I know this year has not been a cakewalk for us, but everything I have railed against comes from a place of love. You decide without feeling—you live on the divide between the head and the heart, following the first without attending to the second. And you know what will come of that? You will break down. Not now. But one day. Perhaps 10 years from now. You will go crazy as your mother did, and when you do, it will be the most silent pain you have ever—"

"Spare me your prophecies," I said. I was weeping and screaming at her, trying to stand, but unable to muster the strength. "Don't talk to me about how I'll end up. You'd just as easily sell yourself out to the highest bidder."

That was the worst thing I had ever said to her. I knew it right away. Her breath disappeared and she looked at me as though I was evolving into a new creature. The apartment was all silent and growing dark because of the lower sun and gathering clouds. A button had been pushed, and it released the vilest thought I had about her: her true man had a 401K, only a presumed interest in art and literature, and was away enough to allow her to be the prized, possible possession of any room she entered. Of course, she slapped me with a force that made my cheek numb. A neighbor yelled in Russian through the wall.

"I have no idea who I'm looking at," she told me. She was both rabid and disconcerted.

She walked into the bedroom and found it anew. I did, too. Those were not our sheets. Those were not our curtains.

With her back to me she said in a low voice, "You are essentially saying you don't love me any longer."

I listened to the words hang in the air.

"I did not say that."

"You don't have to. You said it by slandering me. And now I know how simple it is: we end."

"We end?"

"That is the world I see."

"We can try another go at the therap—"

"I'm not doing that, do you understand? You need to think through each and every facet of your life before you begin to consider how you might possibly, potentially, feel about it. That is not me. Therapy is a waste of my time. You're mistaking me for your ex-girlfriend."

I walked, not stormed, out of the apartment and bought a cup of coffee. The rain was pouring down in heavy sheets, but I didn't care. From across the street I looked up at our building, its simple brick structure, which I so hardly noticed. For over a year, I have entered and exited without looking up, thinking only of our apartment. And now it looks no different from the ones I pass on the subway. Were it not for the number, maybe I would lose it.

The caffeine has moved through me too fast. So

this is what it feels like when love gets supplanted by something just as strong. The rain is picking up, making waterfall splashes on the sidewalk. I just scrolled through the list of contacts on my cell phone but have no idea who to call, what to say. I never thought it would get this bad. There is more to write but I cannot.

28 September

She has left and gone to her parents' house. I opened the door for her at 9:45 this morning. I just managed to put my hand on her shoulder as she rolled her suitcase to the elevator. Her sweatshirt was stained from the crying. Now what?

30 September

Last night, I dreamt of Krakow, where we traveled last spring. In the dream, we were walking through a woodlot spliced with sunlight. The path sloped down a long ravine marked with shrubbery that resembled the bodies of bears. Far away, to the west, a few actual bears lumbered along. We watched them move, their gargantuan bodies marching across moss and dirt. At one instant, we thought the bears spotted us, which caused us to duck behind a tree, filling me with dread and wonder. Once they moved on, we kept down the path that led to a wide opening lined with stripped birch trees and high ferns. The road ahead was undulating toward the sun that soon sank down and in no time a gigantic wash of constellations appeared. A grouping of clear, geometric patterns sprawled through the open sky, and at certain moments, they curved toward a sickled light that was hummed at by hooded men. When the dark broke, the path grew narrow and took us through another woodlot. On the other side, the city of Krakow lay before us, its streetscape swooping below castles and around the Vistula River. We walked through a park run over by dark, green grass still wet and mysterious from the previous night's storm, and then through dusty, empty streets that looked like the southwest of the United States. Up ahead, a beer garden was filled with people talking at a low hum. We sat amongst them and a waiter brought us two tall lagers, which we toasted as we gazed out at the ancient-looking people. I studied her and admired how even her beauty was, how she carried herself, how she was so very much a woman with her idiosyncrasies that were owned, not imitated, that she grew tired and sexy within the same hour, often. Before us, I unfurled a map of central Europe and in no time we were putting our fingers here and there, naming the places we'd go next, which meant in a couple days or many years from now. The church bells sounded their chimes at a low clang, making a far-off noise that seemed to come from the earth itself. Later, as we walked, we encountered a musician circling half-full water glasses in quick succession, making flute sounds into the air. He took us back to his flat, which was a small affair located behind a rusted gate, down an alley of cracked concrete. *This is the famous ghetto and here, only here, I will offer you room and board for one night. After all, one always recognizes a fellow Jew*, he said to her. We accepted without question and placed our bags in the room, atop the twin bed. He led us through the rest of the ghetto and paused over the split concrete that grew sprigs of weeds, winking at me each time. Together, we were frightened and ensorcelled by him, for he was able to walk through the concrete, and one time, he disappeared completely. Fortunately, we found the way back to his flat and slept a terrified sleep, slinging our legs over each other as we dozed, our skin alabaster and new under the blankets. The next day, we traveled to Auschwitz based on the note he left on the counter, and then to the nearby camp, Birkenau. Amid a dozen tourists, a Polish woman led us through the barracks, down the halls lined with photographs of people with shaved heads and numbers, past the room stacked eerily high with children's shoes—most of the them red—past the walls that memorialized nothing, but in that nothingness was the residue of when firing squads snipped away a life. Finally, we arrived at the locked showers, and then to the ovens, which were enormous yet impossible to move within, having such a small opening for—yes, this is where the dead went. She clutched at my hand but I pulled away, because I did not want contact, not with her, not with anyone. A scent began to gather in my nose, and the possibility of what that was almost dragged a mess of vomit straight up my throat. On the bus ride to Birkenau, there were no words between us. We walked in separate directions, her toward the farmhouse-shaped barracks, me toward the woods. A single train track ran to the wood's edge, and behind, chambers I could not see. The grass had grown tall, leaning over the tracks in some places. I gathered a stone and went to place it on the far rock wall, my mouth dry all the while, my heartbeat in my ears. Just then, the land in front of me began to feel off-kilter. At that point, the sounds began. First, it was sonar, but then the frequency went low, into a groan, but not just one groan, very many groans. It wasn't long before I realized: here were the dead. They moved in ways I could not see, but their voices carried through the umber plane. No screams, nothing piercing, the voices of action and inaction, harmony and disharmony filled the air. The ground grew firmer and its color grayed and browned, changing the earth in front of me from left to right, like a sudden cloud wisp over the sun. They were here in this place, perhaps not only the Jews from the 1940s but others too, many generations of people who crossed the field. When I turned around, I couldn't see her. The sounds stopped after a few seconds. And then I left.

[Her]

Finally, he had a job interview this morning. In the six months since he lost his position, I don't know how many applications he has sent out, how many people I've asked for help on his behalf, and still, nothing. It is possible that the man I live with has no sense of the future, and for that reason, I am quite nervous.

Seeing the therapist was a disaster that lasted all of two sessions. She had Buddhist leanings and lectured to us more than listened. The true benefit was not working through our struggles, as her website said. As we sat on the couch, it seemed that the one prescription she made began to echo with us: start writing. No snooping, no need to share it, just write. And so I begin this journal. My hope is to find clarity during this challenging point in my life. I have never been much of a writer, but I believe that there is value in turning away to make sense of what would have no shape otherwise.

I am 31 years old, and for the past year and a half, I have been living far out in Brooklyn with my boyfriend. We moved here because the rent was cheap, because it was unknown to us both, and because it is close to the sea. That is important to me. Most of all, we moved here because anywhere would do, or so we thought, when we decided that our love was such that it required buying a bed together, cooking together, down time together. I do not regret the decision, despite what is happening now: the air is going out of this life and I cannot figure out how to stop it.

Moving has been my condition for so long. My father is a military man who was stationed in Munich, Amsterdam, Half Moon Bay, San Antonio, and now he is retired in upstate New York. Every two or three years, we moved, uprooting ourselves in the night like bandits, oftentimes never saying goodbye to friends, shifting into another ready-made home hundreds of miles away (the rationale for moving military personnel so often has something to do with Pearl Harbor). When you say that you grew up in a military family, people often assume that your father was away in foreign lands busting down doors and ducking from gunfire. Fortunately, that was not the case. He worked as a teacher on the various bases where we lived.

Growing up in such a way makes you aware of how good men can be when etiquette has not been lost. My own brother, Hayden, cared for me and helped raise me with a devotion that is far removed from the squabbles over cell phones and bedroom size that I see on the TV. His sense of being a man was never not admirable. The same can be said of my father. All of this is not to say that such a life is smooth sailing. In fact, you become very aware of how being a nomad is far removed from what many people experience. This is what happened to me when I came to New York. So is it any surprise that I feel on the verge of a breakdown now that the roots I have laid here are disintegrating? What is worse is the feeling that this breakdown will pass, we will end, and then in two years' time, I'll find myself with another lover, perhaps living together, perhaps just sleeping at each other's apartments on occasion. In other words, I am resigned to beginnings and endings. I thought I could put such things to rest when I moved in with him.

It is very difficult to figure out where and when we went awry. Two possibilities come to mind. One was quite a long time ago, last spring, actually. We traveled together to Krakow and then Budapest, some of the loveliest days of my life. Forty-eight hours before we were scheduled to fly home, he announced that he was going to nearby Bratislava to visit his oldest friend, Henry, who was all of a sudden in the area. I was furious, because I sensed the trip had been planned for a long time and he had avoided telling me about it. There are things he won't say to me, things he will only say in the company of his friend. He pressed on that it was not planned, and eventually I gave up and flew back alone. The experience of flying back to the United States by myself, on the heels of such wonder, was awful. For many of those airborne hours, I was certain that I would not know this man for the rest of my life, that once we split, we would never speak again, and likely never pass each other on the street.

The second instance was more recent, and he was not even there. I was working late when several co-workers insisted that we check out early and go to a jazz bar where we could blow off steam. I was hesitant for a few reasons, including who was there and my long, late commute home. But I went anyway, and sure enough, it was trouble. Axel was there, who is a European man a year or two my junior with eyes for me. I don't know where he's from; he's always obtuse when it comes to that question. And he tries so hard around me, to the point that his flirtations enter the realm of goofy, but that's flirtatious to me. Nothing happened between us—I would never allow it—but at one point we were tucked in a far corner of the bar and his hand was on my shoulder. We were very drunk and talking in a low voice, so much so that the sound of our voices could have led elsewhere, regardless of what we were talking about. Did I forget who I was or did I remember who I was? When I arrived home, he was sleeping a deep sleep, so I crawled into bed ever so slowly and pretended I had been there for a long time.

July 29th

In each of the last two mornings, I have awoken to a balloon drifting up. I wonder: how does a balloon lose its holder at six thirty a.m.? Yesterday I kept it to myself, but today I woke him. He lumbered out of sleep when I pointed upward and rubbed his shoulder. The bags under his eyes were like crevices beginning the aging process and his breath smelt wretched. Long ago I didn't think so, but now I do. He leaned on his elbows and we watched the balloon drift east then west, stepping higher with its long trail of a string hanging like a dead snake in the air. Then it went further into the atmosphere and vanished.

Lisette's theory is that this is us at our best. She said that if we stay together, we will only last by waking each other at various hours of the night to point out the latest borealis or moon glow, hoping that the trace of such beauty keeps us going for the rest of the day. That was hard to hear. She is basically saying that how we talk to each other every day isn't good enough. We need to be looking out because we must have decided very long ago that to look at each other isn't sufficient.

It is possible that the land has something to do with this. He grew up a hundred miles outside of Chicago, in a very small town that used to be a farming community. Long ago, it was necessary to keep cordial relations with your neighbors, because you often had to rely upon them for help. The winters were brutal, and you couldn't escape outside. Staying in the house meant keeping your mood at an even keel (My lord, how I have come to hate that term—even keel. Any time he uses it I roll my eyes, and I hope he notices). This makes for a stiffness that lasts up to the present day. He just was not encouraged to express himself. I compare this to me, moving countless times and depending upon the closeness of my family as a source of support, not alienation. Nothing was ever off limits; we spoke to each other from our hearts, not our heads, before the censors got there. I suppose it is a different form of survival.

My father says that you need to look to the physical land one comes from before inviting them into your life. This is a strange thing for him to say, given that my entire family tells a long, wandering story in response to the question *Where are you from?* Yet he is right, as he is about most things. We are ultimately from nowhere, which means that we were never limited to the mores of one place. I know that my mother's Hungarian Jewish ancestry suggests that we were once located somewhere, but the sediment of that in no way lasts to the present day. It is more than a little disheartening that these are the facts of our lives. Often, I imagine him young, out there on that small ranch in Illinois, retreating into himself in ways that worked so well as a child but have no place in the world now.

I said this to my father a few days after we moved in together. He never offered full congratulations. He toasted me up at my parents' house, north of the city, sitting on the porch with the lights out, and warned, "I'm glad you're not rushing to the altar. It takes a long time to know someone." I fell into tears that wouldn't stop, blubbering so much that I spilt my wine. My father got up to fetch a rag, and as he did, he gripped my shoulder and rubbed my head. A few days earlier, I had been so happy about the move-in and then, less than a week later, there I was convinced that I had made the wrong decision. He did his best to console me, but how do you console a daughter whose life course you fundamentally object to? The porch was too dark to tell how upset he was. I just remember him using the term "hemmed in" over my sniffles, which ended after a few minutes and sent me into a deep sleep.

The next day, I rode the Metro North back to Manhattan and walked to Union Square, and then picked up the Q train. It wasn't until the train rose above the ground near Prospect Park that I realized I hadn't lifted my head all day. I had been reading and editing scripts for two films. The work was not consuming enough to get that much of my attention. All at once, the feelings from the last night poured into me and I started sobbing again. As creatures we pick the path of least resistance. Was that what I was doing? Spill my heart, sleep off the effects, and get back to work without changing a thing. This has not always been my custom, but since we moved in

together, it has become something I do, and I hate it.
I hate that I must tend to the cleanup of my own
emotions. He once chided me that my past
relationships have never lasted more than six months.
I said that I have such little patience for accepting an
unhappy station in life. Too many people decide that
love is something they must check off a list in order
to make room for other things. Such as? Dying?
Sleep?

August 3rd

Soon it will be our anniversary, and I cannot
decide whether it is worthwhile to forget it or
celebrate the date with vigor and hope that
remembering it kindles us toward what we once had.
The first night we met, almost two years ago now,
was the greatest evening of my life. I was exhausted
after a long week of filming. A few friends and I
stopped by a bar on Fourth Street between
Lafayette and Bowery around nine p.m. on a
Tuesday night. The place was almost desolate. A
salt-and-pepper haired bartender was reading the
newspaper, sipping a cup of coffee. It was after two
drinks that I saw him, tucked in the corner by the

window, deep into his book. I must have said something to one of my friends about people who read books at bars, and I must have said it loud enough, because he looked up in a not-so-kind way at me. The whole debacle had me red-faced in no time, and considering that I hate to offend strangers, I felt like I had to approach him. So I did, and much to my surprise, he was not as surly as I anticipated. He was reading Garcia Marquez's *One Hundred Years of Solitude*, the opening pages, the part about the discovery of ice. And he was mesmerized by it. I thought that was so wonderful, that this man could be taken by a passage about the discovery of ice, when he came from Illinois, after all. I told him that I was working on an adaptation of a story from Garcia Marquez's *Strange Pilgrims*, and we shared what we liked from that collection. Long ago, he had done a public radio reading of the last story, about the trail of blood in the snow. And when I said that a great heat blazed through me—this is it. We looked around and the bar was about to close. My friends had left a long time before without telling me. We weren't even drunk; we actually did not have a single drink together. We talked in the kindest confessions ever spoken until our mouths ran dry. It was two a.m. by the time we walked out into the street, which was warm and comforting. He lived with a roommate several blocks east, in an illegal sublet, and we walked that way without ever pausing over the question of whether I would spend the night. I did. There was no sex. There was only a long, uninterrupted kiss before sunrise when we fell asleep, fully clothed, facing each other. To myself, I said that I loved him when I got on the train at Bleecker Street a few hours later.

At what point this stops being a horrible memory, I don't know. It is horrible because I am fundamentally opposed to the way things are, but the press of those few hours exerts such a weight on me, I cannot bear it at times. Now I watch him iron his pants and try, fail, and try again to knot a tie through his only white button-down shirt. To me, what he imagines the world to be is opaque.

August 10th

Let's see, what did I find upon scrolling through our computer's browsing history today as I tried to fetch a curry recipe? Thirty clicks through Nina's Facebook photos, questions posed to WebMD about bipolar disorder, and news websites. Many

times I have told him that if he wants to look at
pictures of his ex-girlfriend, do so. It is how he does
these things that drives me mad, for it is secretive.
Early on, my father taught me that I must judge
men by what they show me, and not guess at what
they intend.

My problem with Nina is not that I believe he is
still in love with her. I know she had drug problems,
asked for the attention of other men for kicks, and
for reasons unknown, fled to Vancouver. That is the
story I am told. But it is the story of what they
fought about when they split, and not the story of
what their lives together was like. I know they were
quite happy, and I know that he found her
enchanting. Before she left for the west, she asked
him to come with her, and he almost did. Distance
made for the break, which means that were it not
for that, it is possible they would still be together. I
remember that awful night three months into our
relationship when we made the mistake of telling
each other everyone we have been with. I care none
at all that he's slept with two dozen others. So have
I. But I remember how obtuse he was when he
described her. To me, it meant that he could not
express the depth of phone calls, nights spent
together, the meals shared. Every time afterward

when he began to talk about that period in his life, he stopped himself. I can only guess he stopped himself because he was afraid I would think it overshadowed the present. Or he was afraid that in telling me, I would see how she touched every facet of his life and added to the man I see now. This has always been my hope: the time before us can dissolve.

August 15th

It is three a.m. and I am still awake, accepting that no sleep will happen tonight. We have been at each other's throats brutally for the last two days. As is often the case, it takes almost nothing to prompt a fight. Ever since the film premiere, he has hurled countless questions after me about Axel. These are not baseless, but I also don't deserve the third degree. Last night I arrived home late, and by the time I got here, he was back from an outing with Henry, drunk already and keeping at it. On the military base as a child, I would meet women whose husbands were angry alcoholics. The thought of ever ending up with such a man was so alien to me. Why would they stay? Not to exaggerate—my situation is not that bad. But I do see how men become drunk and zero their hate at the woman in the room who remains convinced that this will pass. When I first knew him, he would get sentimental after a few drinks, and often very funny. Now it becomes a way to get rid of the censor.

Out the window, I see the Verrazano bridge, a huge feat of engineering. We used to pretend that the red lights atop the bridge were radio towers, and that gave us solace during the first few months we were here. I also see the fire station across the street, the thin line of metal from the aboveground subway, and the lone bodega with the dulled blue lettering. We wanted to live somewhere quiet. It has always been important to me to feel elsewhere. For him, I don't think it matters. In the smallest ways, he lacks conviction because so little has been up for grabs in his life.

I think of Krakow. The reason why we traveled there was a dream, and back then I thought dreams could lead your life in fated directions. He agreed in a heartbeat, because he had never been to Europe. We flew to Poland and took a long bus ride to the city, through the strange hillsides outside Krakow, which looked uninhabited in the way I bet many European hamlets looked centuries before. From the moment our plane touched down, we seemed to

forget how to speak to each other. But that makes it
sound unpleasant, and that is not at all what it was.
In Poland, we fell into the perfect silence of co-
presence. Even disembarking and getting lost near a
swirling highway didn't throw us. We made our way
along the oval park that lined the city, the gnarled
benches black with rainwater that somehow lifted us.
Then we found our hostel through a courtyard so
gray we might as well have been in an etching. The
sheets on the small bed were dusty and the pillows
were flat, and the tapestry that lay at the foot of the
bed was rich with colors and shapes that swirled like
the highway we had just seen. From that moment,
out into the long, bright air, we were other people. I
don't mean that we pretended we were other people,
or that the troubles in our lives were absent. I mean
that our names and histories slid away, and for four
days, what was left was love between us.

That Krakow showed wounds from the war
amazed me. I could not stop photographing the
shattered concrete and the grass that mysteriously
grew around it. We refused to drink much during
our time there because it felt wrong to do so. This,
like so much, we didn't even need to say. The
Hasidic reggae rapper Matisyahu staged a concert
one night in the ghetto, drawing an enormous

crowd more pensive than any I had ever seen. We searched for a good vantage, but no matter how hard we tried, we could not see him, we could only see his image projected on the screens they set up. So he said that we should enter an apartment building and ask one of the residents if we could watch the concert from their terrace. What?! This idea was impossible to me. How would we ask? Neither of us spoke Polish. Besides, shouldn't we just enjoy what we were hearing? But he said no, and before I knew it, we managed to slide past the front door of a six story building, where we began to climb the steps until the third floor, where he said, "Here, let's try here," with an expression on his face that I had never seen before. His brown hair was looser and sweeping across his forehead. Finally, here was someone who knew what he wanted, absurd as it was. He walked to the end of the hall and I trailed behind him, excited and full of shame at the same time. He knocked and an old man opened the door completely, looking suspicious and soon angry. I don't know what he said, how he convinced him, but before I knew it, we were spreading three lawn chairs onto the terrace three flights above the stage, looking down onto the head of Matisyahu. It was incredible, one of the most incredible hours of my life, because there was no way we were supposed to be there, no way that circumstances should have played out like this. The man who lived there did not talk much; perhaps he thought we would rob him in due time. But he did hand us two beers, and then he took out one for himself, and we toasted the beers together. The songs drifted through me; I didn't know the musician very well, and except for his slower songs, which sounded like laments, I wasn't very interested. My skin felt smooth and new, and for some reason, the air was saturated with the smell of lavender. I was more interested in how the men next to me felt at home in the world. This is what we were all meant to do, and we were doing it. Here I am writing about this many months later, and I wonder how much perfection this moment had when it was happening. I don't think it is different than how I am remembering it.

Now I am in the kitchen boiling water for the tea. The dishes lay in the sink from last night's curry, a few of my photographs hang on the slim sections of wall, and artifacts like sticks and pinecones are arranged. He brought these home one day from Prospect Park. He forages for these things and never tells me what they mean to him. The light in here is horrid; it is that vast, dull yellow that fills most New York kitchens, so I only have the light on above the stove for the time being. A few beads of rain have slipped into the screen and brushed against the plant. The table that I am at is one of the few things he carried with him from Illinois; he and his father varnished it the day before he drove here. Then they drank beer and walked in the woods until it grew dark, saying things he never knew about his Scottish ancestors, most of them sailors.

I have heard this story many times.

I wish he would make more of an effort with my father. I can't help but feel that this is part of the problem right now, and truthfully, it has always been part of the problem. He knows that I am disappointed in how he doesn't try, yet he won't talk about it. I don't know what I hope, but I hope for better than what I see. When he is around my father, he defers and looks away, laughs when he is supposed to laugh, says just enough in conversation to meet some invisible social standard. After two years, he must understand that the bloodline tying my clan together is very thin. Most are dead or estranged. Can he understand what that is like? My brother always says that women hail from a place more ancient than men. This means that piety is essential to who we are. I understand this and accept this, but why the man I love does not is a mystery to me. The first time they met was at a hospital when my father was being discharged following a minor knee operation. Given, that is not the most ideal circumstance to meet someone. But he just stood there! Asking banal questions about how his leg was, what the hospital was like. This is my partner at his worst: a staccato series of closed-ended questions to fill the empty space. All I wanted to do was crawl under the table and nap for 75 years.

Sometimes when the three of us have dinner together, we are laughing and it is wonderful, but then there is this terrible silence that follows, where everyone's feelings seem to be laid bare.

It is easier for him to talk about Axel. Is this how men regard their shortcomings? Do they imagine right away the others you will make love with in their absence? The terrible irony of this situation is that Axel only becomes a problem when he talks about him as one. Sure, there was that evening many months back when I am afraid that I gave him the wrong impression. But that idiot flirts with everyone, and he is so very boyish, I can't imagine a grown woman getting wrapped up in all that. The evening of the film premier, I knew the rage was coming when he saw Axel resting his hand on my shoulder. And it did. As much as I tried to pull him away and show these strangers my boyfriend, all he did was lean against the wall and get drunk with a cynical Australian man named Jean-Paul (Jean-Paul actually put his hand on my hip for a long time when I met him the month before! He was glassy eyed and rocking back and forth, capable of anything). Good god, they must have had a dozen beers each. It was eking out of their pores by the time they sat down. And it didn't help that the film was a bust. The slight work I did was positive, perhaps, but who knows. He never really told me what he thought about it, just as he has never really told me what he thinks about anything I've made.

He carted that idiot Jean-Paul with us all the way back to Midwood, staring at me, avoiding any question I asked him.

"Can you just talk to me?" I asked him, somewhere around Prospect Park.

"About what? What is there to possibly say?"

He had never been so cutting with me, and I wondered if his question was right. There's no way he was actually holding a grudge over Axel. I know him too well. He was angry that I made something without him. Even his body said it. Usually he stands so straight, which makes him seem taller than he is. But at the premiere, I could see him hunch, his stomach extended and his neck tilted ever so slightly. His arms were crossed tight. This means that he does not want to be himself. Am I to feel guilty about this? I shouldn't. A woman approached me at the ABC No Rio Art Fair a year ago saying she liked my photographs and would I like to do some work on a film. I said yes, did a little work, and received a pittance for it.

It is quarter to five right now and the sky is changing, the building across the street is growing pink. My body is so heavy and tired. A bass far off pounds, and I cannot imagine why and how someone is listening to music that loud at this hour. Good for them. This is the most peace I have felt in a long time.

September 2nd

I had hoped that by not writing in this journal, my life would improve. And I was right! This is the opposite of what the therapist said, for all the good came when we weren't knee-deep in words and reflection. In fact, it was through a weekend of labor that we began to resemble people who love each other.

Those who lived here before us left a few gallons of paint under the sink, a shade of yellow between mustard and gold. It was not ideal, but in these thin times, we tend to accept anything that comes free. We dragged out the rollers, the brushes, the drop cloth, and off we went. He made sure to play that Dylan album he thinks so much of, and before long, I was hypnotized. First, we spackled the ceiling and walls and then we sat on the floor, waiting for it to dry. He went over to the desk and thumbed through a whole series of photographs I took when we first moved in. I went over to him and leaned on his shoulder as he looked. His hair was much shorter in those days and mine was much longer, and he had no lines under his eyes. He complimented me on the photographs and spoke about their technical aspects. I had no idea he regarded them at all, no idea why he decided to look at them just then. Many were pictures I had taken at Coney Island, some portraits of him, miscellany from the neighborhood.

When we got undressed and laid down on the drop cloth, it was the first time I could remember wanting to sleep with him in many months. The loss of his job and the problems we faced since last winter have made it so I often wonder if he is attracted to me, and because I wonder, I pull back from him. The therapist posed to us this very strange question: Under what circumstances do you want each other? Now, I would answer: where there is some indication that he is certain about what he says and what he wants in the world. When his concentration is keen, when it doesn't flit around, I see someone I want very much.

By the time we finished, I felt goofy. He went to work on the first coat and I rode the elevator downstairs to fetch two sandwiches from the bodega. Ella, the Israeli woman who runs the counter, said I looked happy. "Smiling in the style of long ago," she said. I looked down and realized my tank-top was inside out. She noticed it as well and smirked as she averted her eyes.

I walked under the awning of the dialysis center and the small medical plaza. Obese women with strollers stared at me. An older man with a tube for oxygen lining his nose nodded through the window. As I crossed to go home, I paused in the middle of the street, and looked behind me, where the avenue opened wide to make an esplanade full of trees with verdant leaves and buildings set six stories high, all the same mortar color. The green and the brown made so much of the past six months slide away.

There were colors of the earth, high up in the sky.

Upstairs, we ate our sandwiches where we had just made love. I asked him if he was still committed to producing the radio program he talked about earlier in the summer. He made a wavering motion with his mouth as he chewed, and then we got back to work.

September 11th

Thirteen years ago today, I was a senior in high school, sitting in my physics class on a sleepy Tuesday morning. Across the hall, I could see the black hair of the civics teacher flail. Before the end of the period, he brought into our room a television on a roller with NBC news coverage. The World Trade Center smoldered. A second plane had hit the other tower, making it clear that it was intentional, not an air traffic accident.

I ran out of the room and sprinted to the phone near the administrative office. I dialed Hayden's cell phone but there was no answer. Straight to voicemail. I phoned my parents and their lines were busy. So I tried again, and again, until finally it rang. No, they said, we haven't heard from him. We're trying like mad. We don't know. Keep phoning him. Please, please.

My brother was headed to Los Angeles for a job interview. The previous spring, he had graduated college with a focus in architecture. A firm in Los Angeles paid for him to fly in for an interview. He was living in Boston at the time, so his flight left from Logan, which meant—

The school secretary was watching the impact videos online. I watched, too, from behind the sectioned glass, not sure if I was seeing my brother reduced to dust. Not an instant felt real. In fact, it was only when I saw small black specks—people— fall from a great height that it began to feel real. How was that so? They were jumping out of a building because of what was now in the building. I stood there with the phone against my cheek making its horrid sound. Entrapment in iron made me think of our first bath, but I didn't want to think of it. The secretary saw me looking and turned down the sound. A David Brinkley type was about to say how radicalization happened. A boy ran by shouting, Tuesday bloody Tuesday.

I didn't hang up the phone, didn't go back to class. I began to walk home, which was two miles away. I remember that the sky was severe blue but the air felt cold, so I kept my arms folded across my chest the whole way, leaning forward and tripping at times. Nothing in San Antonio said what was happening. My parents were still at work, so I sat cross-legged on the rug and turned on the television. The buildings were still burning; the newscasters were quiet. The way the light came in through the front door made the dust in the air so clear, little cartwheels of bits and pieces that were coming into our lungs, and we had no idea. At that, I fell into another weeping fit, so full that I was almost sick, thinking of what could be in his lungs. When the heaving stopped, I went into my father's study and looked at his strange collection of books, many of which were philosophy and religion. The ideas he thought of often but never talked of were scattered about.

A car engine went off, and then another a few seconds later. My parents arrived home. My father's face darkened as soon as he stepped in. He didn't make eye contact with me; he went over to the sink, turned it on, ran his hands under the water, and let them drip on the floor. My mother took off to the bathroom right away, turned on the faucet, and fell into a deep crying fit of her own. No one spoke to anyone. It was impossible that this was happening. I tried Hayden's number again but there was no answer, so I went back to the television and watched the news coverage for a few minutes. This time it made a numb feeling stretch from my head to my hip. One of the buildings fell away, becoming a huge cloud of gray that slid to the earth. I put my hands over my mouth and bit the insides of my cheeks to keep from screaming. My father paused at the other end of the hallway, watching me, and then he went upstairs. He wouldn't come in and see what was happening. Katie Couric and Matt Lauer tried to say something. They took turns speaking.

The phone rang, making me shriek, with the ringer so loud it seemed as though it would bust the sound barrier. Hayden. He called and said that he was late and didn't make it through security. He had overslept. It was like the first and thousandth time hearing his voice. My heart was in my throat, never so warm.

September 15th

Right now, my lover is in another country. He went to Montreal with his oldest friend, supposedly tagging along for a conference. In so many ways, he is more cut out to be with the men in his life than any woman.

Once I finished bartending, I was exhausted but feeling free since he was away, so I went to the Brandy Library in Tribeca. I walked in and sat down, ordered an Oban, and enjoyed the single time in my life that I was in a bar alone. At first, I thought I would make it through the night unbothered, but then the young banker two seats down gave me the eyes and said, "You look confused." This, I have learned, is how men come to ingratiate themselves to women. By offense. I simply responded, "No" and went back to my drink without ever looking in his direction again. Another guy ordered a drink by nudging into me and apologizing, as though his apology was enough to evoke my life's tale. Before long, I shook my head and took my drink to the far corner of the bar, where I sat at a small table that faced the street. Clean drizzle had started that balanced just above the height of umbrellas. A man loved me several hundred miles away, and soon he would be back, and despite our troubles, we were in it for the long haul. That is what I said under my breath.

The train ride back to Midwood was very long. It was one of those rides where there are no words or expressions shared between the people on the train, just a series of bumps and beeps, bodies shuffled back and forth. The walk from the subway to our apartment was more deserted than ever. I didn't see a single person out for a long time, only two plastic bags rolling through the streets like urban tumbleweed. Perhaps it was the exhaustion, or the Oban on an empty stomach, but I didn't go home. I kept walking past our apartment, further down Ocean Avenue, where the drizzle kept up. Were he to learn about this, or my father or brother, I would never hear the end of it. Finally, I saw an old woman coming toward me who looked as though she had emerged from Ellis Island a hundred years ago. A few blocks away, I could hear the gigantic churl of the subway curving toward Coney Island. And in that instant, it was the most pleasure I had known since Krakow. It was the same feeling of sliding away.

Soon, I came to the edge of Manhattan Beach. The sea looked green, like a suspenseful film, and the mist over the surf was made blurry by the lights that projected their sheen out on the water. I took off my sandals and walked onto the sand. To the right, a few rides from Coney Island stayed lit. That I couldn't see all of the water overwhelmed me, and I had to steady myself to make sure I was not in it already. Since the sand was damp, I wasn't sure, so I extended my leg ever so slowly to see what was ahead. And as I did so, I realized I was lying down, and what I was seeing above was just gray, a haze drifting like cigarette smoke. The water began to pool under my back, then up to my neck. I saw myself in a painting, a large horizontal canvas from long ago, a woman who lays recumbent in the forest as it changes above her. There is no one else in the painting. The cypress trees hang over her, so many that they make a steepled shape as far as the eye can see. Rocks that guard her let in a slow creek.

September 23rd

Today I woke up to new light, new sounds from the people above, and a skyline of trees if I lean my head out the living room window. I am in Lisette's apartment, curled up on the couch with her blue throw over me. It is six a.m. My mouth is dry from the two bottles of Cote-du-Rhone that we drank last night. It is never a good idea to take a final swig of wine and then fall into a heavy sleep a minute later.

This is what happened: he got home late from his trip to Montreal, he walked around the apartment like a ghost, not coming into the bedroom right away. I was in and out of sleep, so I didn't realize how long he spent in the living room, sitting in the dark. Three hours for god's sake. The next day, I was up early to photograph a portrait session in the city. By the time I left the apartment, he was still dead to the world on the far side of the bed with no sheets atop him. When I got home, he was still pacing, with so much on his mind. I hugged him and asked him what the matter was, and he said, without any prompting, that he did not think we should be together any longer. The sentence had been said so much in his head it did not even sound true when it came out. He might as well have hit me, for I retched back toward the couch.

"What do you mean?" I asked him.

"I kissed a woman in Montreal. It wasn't intentional, but it happened."

"You kissed a woman?! Who?"

"A stripper. I was quite drunk when I did it, but that's beside the point."

"You're right that's beside the point. What is wrong with you?"

Nothing on earth prepared me for that. And even as I was stunned, I could picture it. I know how he reacts to attention. That was the horrible moment, the instant when I began to imagine what he was like when I was not around.

"These two things have nothing to do with each other," I told him, holding my hips to stay steady. He looked at me as though he did not understand. "Nothing. You know that, right? Us being together has nothing to do with you kissing a stripper."

"No," he said, without explaining himself. "I have to tell you, too, that I have been communicating with Nina. I have to be honest. And now I have doubts."

I might as well have broken my collarbone. The pain since then has been constant. I went into the kitchen and smashed the first wine glass I could find, because why not? And then I came here. Lisette gave me a key to her apartment many months ago in the event this happened, and lo and behold, it did. I walked in without knocking and she was slung on the couch, in her sweatpants, looking like the most casual woman in all of history.

"Hey stranger," she said. "You look like you need a shoulder."

I cried against her. The tears were so endless I didn't know how they would stop. And I believed at once that part of what ripped my insides out was how casually she was spending her evening, how this would soon be my evening, that no matter how hard I resisted, I would have to concede that she was right. He was not for me.

I am safe in case you're wondering, I texted him later on.

Good, he said.

Good? That was all.

What I admired about her apartment was that she only hung original artwork on the walls. A few of my photographs, some inexpensive work she had purchased at the ABC No Rio Fair, a gift from a wealthy relative. The people that she paid homage to were alive. There were many things I did not understand about her, such as how she worked every day as a nanny for an investment banker just north of the city, why she didn't care to get out of it, how she had given up on being in love.

*   *   *

Right now it is four p.m. and my body is sore from a long bicycle ride in Prospect Park. Lisette took her bicycle, and I borrowed her neighbor's, and we rode for over an hour around the circuit. To get there we had to cross the Grand Army Plaza. The long promenade was slow and hazy and completely out of place. Every time I looked at it, I imagined that I was lost in a foreign city.

For no more than eight minutes was it possible

to imagine that he didn't exist. That is what I wanted. I wanted to subtract him from my life, but then every eight minutes, it became clear that it was not possible. It was then, on a bicycle riding up a rise in Prospect Park, that I began to get a sense of what I was in for. Many places in Brooklyn had enormous intersections that were the spout for major highways, and often they were uncluttered, until a big rush of traffic filled them up. Seeing that was always disappointing to me. I hoped that such places could stay empty, even if that meant they were ghostly. There was no way around it: he was saying no to me, and to a life. Perhaps he had just gotten a jump on what would have happened anyway. Lisette smiled at me and kept riding, at which point I saw that she didn't have a helmet, and neither did I. With the wrong turn of events, we could both die from head trauma if we crashed. But that didn't matter one bit.

We braked for water atop the steepest climb in the park and looked around at the trees, which were still green. I reached for my phone and sent him a text message.

I'm in the park on a bicycle.

Good.

Is that all you say—good? Have you become an off-the-boat immigrant since I left?

No and stop. I'm happy for you.

Why are you happy for me? I'm miserable.

Maybe you're getting what you need.

What are you doing?

Job searching.

Please tell me you're doing something other than that. I am not sleeping there right now. Can you please not proceed as though it's business as usual?

It's urgent. Why shouldn't I?

I put the phone away when she looked at me, and I nodded to her that I was good for another lap. The way the wind played against my face made it possible that all could be livable, not renewed or repaired. We rode our bicycles close to each other, and she asked me practical questions such as where I would live and if I needed help looking for apartments.

I pulled the bicycle over because my heart was going too fast. She shook her head as though she was responsible for all this when all she was trying to do was help. Lisette was right. There were so many moments I had bypassed. How my father's expression did not change when I told him of our plans to live together. Lisette's meek congratulations. Many times I would be running an errand—maybe in the pharmacy—and I would wonder for a moment why I didn't tell more people, why there were even some people in my life who didn't know he existed. Then I would go home and forget about it altogether.

As I said these things to her, I looked down at my hands, and I was tearing up big chunks of grass that stained my palms a light brown-green. She sat with me and did the same, as though my life were anything to follow. I looked away from her through a patch of trees that were thick enough to make me forget where I was. Lisette did her best to pull me out of it by talking about a disastrous date she had gone on last week. The guy brought with him a small peanut butter sandwich with magic mushrooms he ate within five minutes of arriving at the bar. She stuck around purely for the sake of entertainment when the drugs kicked in.

"Oh, no," I said. "I can't do that."

"The real bummer is that courts compute alimony based on projected income, not actual income," she said to me.

"What?"

"If you had gone through with marriage eventually, and then divorced. On paper it looks like he could make a lot of money, so you would have been slowly bleeding him dry for a long time. You could always reconcile and take that route," and then she lifted her shoulders in a shrug.

"That's horrible, I never want to do that. I never want to drag the end of my relationship through court."

"That's what plenty of people say, and then they do it."

"Fine, let them. We don't have children; we don't own property. Almost everything we share was found."

"Then it will be easy."

October 3rd

I feel as though people have gone underground and the trees are slanted ever so slightly out the window. If I stare too long at my hands, I see the places where the blood looks close to the surface.

* * *

That was last night. I feel better now, though sometimes when I am taking a step, it seems like the ground has dropped an inch or two, like an unexpected stair, and I trip. Hayden says that this is part of the anxiety, and it will go away, but right now it is acute. He also says that it is important that I don't stare for too long. This morning he caught me doing that from the porch and snapped his finger close to my ear.

Where else can I be but here? I spent several nights at Lisette's, but I was only putting off the inevitable by staying. I did go back to Midwood and it was even worse than when I left. He tried to make love to me in the shower. When I gave him a look of horror, as though I had never seen him before, he turned away. And then we talked. Rather, I talked at him. He still had nothing to say, no explanation. I wish there was something on earth to prepare me for my partner's silence. I could not—and still can't—believe that this is happening. It makes sense to me because things have been so bad for so long, yet it is also impossible.

I slept there that night, me in the bed, him on the couch. There is no etiquette for endings, so when in doubt, default to what you see on the TV. A night of torrid dreams came: drowning, electronics dissolving.

We did not speak in the morning at first. We went about our business. He made his coffee, I packed a suitcase. Then I told him I was leaving and he said, "That's for the best right now. When will you be back?" No pause between the sentences. I could have forgiven those words had he paused between those two thoughts, paused and considered how bad it had gotten. It was as though we were talking about groceries. Part of me hates him.

The Metro North was uncrowded. I heaved my suitcase on the holder above but didn't have the strength, and it came crashing down on my foot. The conductor came over and helped me lift it, tucked it in to make sure that wouldn't happen again, and gave me a ticket I didn't pay for. I don't think I said anything to him. I don't know what he looked like.

Was anyone alive in the mid-morning? The train went past the derelict parts of Harlem and the Bronx. Hardly any cars were out as we passed the backs of a lot of buildings. Some of the graffiti was funny.

Hayden picked me up the train station. When I came around the post, I saw his red Taurus idling in the parking lot, and I sat down on a bench instead of going over to him. It was fine to stay on the train, in an empty car, or walk by strangers, because then it could stay unreal. The train revved and pulled away with its high-pitched hiss and I put my face in my hands. The gravel below on the tracks shook a little then went back to its place. He would come find me soon, thinking he got my arrival time wrong. And he did. I knew he was there before I saw him.

He scraped his shoe against the platform's concrete to announce himself. My brother was always mistaken for being from another country and he looked more like that than ever. His posture is so strange. Depending on whom he's speaking to, he can either seem very tall or hunched, because I think he tries to meet the other person as closely as possible. He also has a looseness to his body that a lot of American men don't have. Soon his hand was on my shoulder, giving it a squeeze, and then he popped the pull on my suitcase and began to roll it toward the car. I followed, dragging my feet across the platform and not saying anything to him, not even bothering with sunglasses. He kept his hand on my shoulder and went into a long tangent about family history he had dug up as the car inched in reverse. His research brought him as far back as the sixteen hundreds in what is now Hungary, a town that does not exist any longer. I can't remember the name. In the next breath, he asked how I was and then chided himself for even asking.

"I'm still here," I said.

My parents were away visiting my father's brother, though now they are on their way back.

* * *

Why am I still writing in this? I have not re-read a single entry since I started. The therapist said that I should read through the journal every few days to get a "history of [my] emotions," and "become a more reflective person." That is a terrible idea. When we started dating, he saved every voicemail I left him. Most of them were logistical (I have never been elegant over the phone). "I'll meet you here in an hour." "Give me a call. I have an idea for what to cook." "What is the name of that photographer I said I liked?" It drove me mad that he saved these, because after a while his voice mailbox was so full I could not leave a new message! He claimed that when I wasn't there he would listen to the messages. Once this made me happy. Now I hate it. Why keep listening to something someone said once?

* * *

It had been 13 years since we were in the house by ourselves. Since then, Hayden was always gone. And when he was home, I was gone. We so rarely intersected as adults, though we stayed close. Loving each other did not entail seeing each other in the flesh.

On the couch, I wrapped all the blankets around me and told him what happened. He nodded and bit his lip, lowered his head, rubbed his hands. He started to tell me about a bad breakup of his own, but I was so numb that it must have been vibrating from my core, for he stopped himself. We looked around at our parents' house, the artifacts from the countries and states where we lived. Our father and mother were so slight when it came to showing their geographies. Everything—their couch, the antique-looking desk, the heavy mirror with an oak frame— these things had been with us for a long time, always in the same place.

The only thing to do was drink. Hayden cooked me dinner, curry actually, which outshined the curry I had made weeks earlier. With it, we drank South American wine our father had brought from a trip there long ago, expensive stuff that stayed in my mouth and made me think of where the flavors came from. The past week has been so drenched in wine for me. After one bottle, we had another, which made a new, numb feeling mainly in my head. I knew I was deep in because the ends of my fingers began to feel rubbery, the sensation going away from them. I said this to Hayden.

"Where does it go?"

"Inside," I said back in a goofy voice, tapping my fingers in the air.

He laughed and opened a third bottle. Now the

taste had vanished and I was just drinking because he was. We walked through the house based on what things we remembered and could still identify from Half Moon Bay, which was our favorite of any of the locations we lived. Then we stopped talking but kept moving through the house. Where our parents lived was so quiet. Because of that quiet, I could hear my brother breathe and I thought, how strange that I can hear a man breathe.

*   *   *

I was 16 when we lived in Half Moon Bay and Hayden was 20, also living at home and commuting to the local college as a non-matriculated student. This was the week before we moved. He knew how I would go out at night and perch on a tree at the far end of our property that let me hear the sea. I didn't care how trite it was. I had been landlocked for a good deal of my childhood, so being near an ocean was one of the best and realest things that ever happened to me. From the right branch, I could even glance the ocean, but it was night, so there was nothing to see. And it was perfect like that.

We had a big jug of Carlo Rossi wine that night that we would go back to every few minutes. I wasn't even certain that he was asleep when I left, around twelve-thirty, my usual time. Because our parents were away that evening, I didn't bother closing the door lightly. It swung shut, and he must have heard me. But I had on a long buzz, so there wasn't anything to think of besides the two hundred or so feet between the house and the small trees up a rise. I didn't hear him behind me. I don't know how long he was standing there. When I climbed down the tree, he looked like a ghost, his face whiter than ever and his eyes a spring green color that was clear even through the dark. I asked if he wanted to come up and see what I saw. He shook his head and looked away, drifting in his stance. He came up to me and his breath smelt hot, wine hot, and a small purple ring outlined the high part of his lip. I remember wondering what if?

October 7th

I am mailing this journal to him with the hope that he reads this letter, if nothing else. I never failed to show you who I am. Take it.

* * *

I know how you flip to the last page of any book

you consider buying not because you want to see its length, as you say, but because you want to see how it ends, caring so much more for how the writer gets there rather than any final reveal. Once you know how it ends, you are freer to live in its intricacies. It is not out of the question that you will read this first, and depending on how it goes, never bother with the rest. So be it. This is what I have long meant by showing yourself to me. I doubt you would lay yourself bare in this way.

The past several days have been the worst of my life. When I saw my parents, I went 24 hours without telling them what had happened. I knew that once I did, this would be over. I pretended to be sick, but I'm not a good liar. Eventually, I could not pretend to sleep and keep the door closed, so I told them two days ago. Right now, I can only communicate with one person at a time. Being around several people at once, even family, makes me feel like I am drowning. So they have been taking turns asking me what I need. It is strange that I don't have an answer to that question, that I need nothing. I feel like an alien. I feel like I am watching Earth from up high.

If you fear that we are upstate making a dartboard with your face as the bull's-eye, you're wrong. They feel quite bad for you and are worried about you. Wherever you are, whatever you are doing right now, I hope that you are not shut up in our apartment with your heart beating through your chest, drenched in sweat, and pacing. I hope you are talking to someone. And if that means going back to that dreaded therapist, then do it.

You said on the morning that I left that you could not be with me in good faith. We must be on firm footing, with our heads clear, knowing one hundred percent what we are getting into. These were your words. What you are essentially saying is that one must know the other person completely and have a perfect map of what is to come. But in saying that, you are giving yourself an out, because I know so well how much you relish mystery. You never want to know others completely. You have some rationale for this that I don't understand. So you have made this bind for yourself where you say one thing but truly want another.

The terrible thing is that I have come to agree with you. There is no way we can be together. If you honestly believe that I will move back in and we will continue in a relationship, you are not dealing with reality.

Not once during our go arounds this summer did I think that you were unsure about us being together.

You must have been unsure for quite some time. That is what worries me. I know you hold inside of you many worlds that you do not want to show to me, and this is one of them. If you think that I would spend my days walking down the street in silent anger, holding hands, you are crazy. What sort of life is that? Promise me that you will seek out help in the time to come. As much as I don't want to see you right now, I also don't want the worst for you.

I must take care of myself. I quit the portrait work I was commissioned to do because I cannot manage to leave the house. The other job— photographing that wedding—I also backed out of, because how could I possibly attend such an event? You do realize that I am losing money now, right? "Everyone you meet is facing a hard battle." You say that a lot without meaning it. You cannot enter other people's struggles, not even the ones of the woman you love.

Consider what happens next. I will move out. I don't know what you will do. Perhaps you will find a job and then a roommate. Perhaps you will go home and live with your father. I will be up here for the next two weeks, at which point I would like to have the apartment to myself for the weekend to pack and move. Other than my clothes and books, I won't be taking much. Keep the furniture that we found and the bed. I will mail you a rent check that tends to my share of October. Contact the landlord soon and inform him that we are breaking the lease. My parents will tend to fees if there are any, but I don't think there will be.

It is six p.m. and I have my father's army blanket over me. Up here, the leaves are beginning to get their color. A part of me wishes you were here now. On the porch railing, a cardinal just landed a moment ago and stared me in the face, turning its beak left and right. It is strange that I have never looked much at birds. Their small bodies, with the black spots that look like flecks of paint, are incredible. You probably know that when I was a child, I went to a funeral of a family friend who died after a bout with leukemia. As the coffin was lowered to the earth, my mother pointed to a cardinal that zoomed back and forth above the crowd, and said, "That is where people go."

I will not sit here and demand that you love me and change your mind. What person wants to bleat like a sheep? You are not the man I want. To write that, to say that out loud, moves all the organs in my body. Perhaps we will find each other again, but perhaps not.

Acknowledgements

I appreciate the following contributions to this work quite deeply: historical research by Peter Haas into the moods of Krakow; early readership by Mark Nickels, Andrew McCarron, and Max Dorfman that proved vital; careful, insightful editing by Carrie Bond; an aesthetically pleasing cover design by Robin Kemkes; and moral support by Arlo the dog and Juni the dog.

More books from
Harvard Square Editions:

People and Peppers, Kelvin Christopher James

Gates of Eden, Charles Degelman

Love's Affliction, Fidelis Mkparu

Transoceanic Lights, S. Li

Close, Erika Raskin

Anomie, Jeff Lockwood

Living Treasures, Yang Huang

Nature's Confession, J.L. Morin

A Face in the Sky, Greg Jenkins

Dark Lady of Hollywood, Diane Haithman

How Fast Can You Run, Harriet Levin Millan

Growing Up White, James P. Stobaugh

The Beard, Alan Swyer

Parallel, Sharon Erby

Dear Reader, I would love to hear your thoughts
on my book. If you enjoyed this book,
please leave a review!